First to the Top

Contents

	Page
Edmund Hillary	2-3
Tenzing Norgay and the Sherpas	4-5
Special gear	6-7
Climbing	8-9
Strongest climbers	10-11
Last try	12-13
At the top	14-15
World news	16

written by Diana Freeman

Edmund Hillary was a young man who lived in New Zealand.
He liked climbing high mountains.
In 1953, he went to Nepal to climb the highest mountain in the world.

Mt. Everest

Hillary was with a team of climbers who all wanted to go to the top of Mt. Everest. They were helped by men called Sherpas, who lived in Nepal.
Tenzing Norgay was a strong Sherpa.

Sherpas

They made a camp with tents on the snow.
The climbers had special clothes to keep them warm and dry.
They had ice axes and strong ropes.
They needed snow goggles and boots with spikes.

7

When the weather was right, the men climbed higher and higher all day.
They made new camps as they went up.
Sometimes there were snowstorms.
Then they had to wait in the camps.

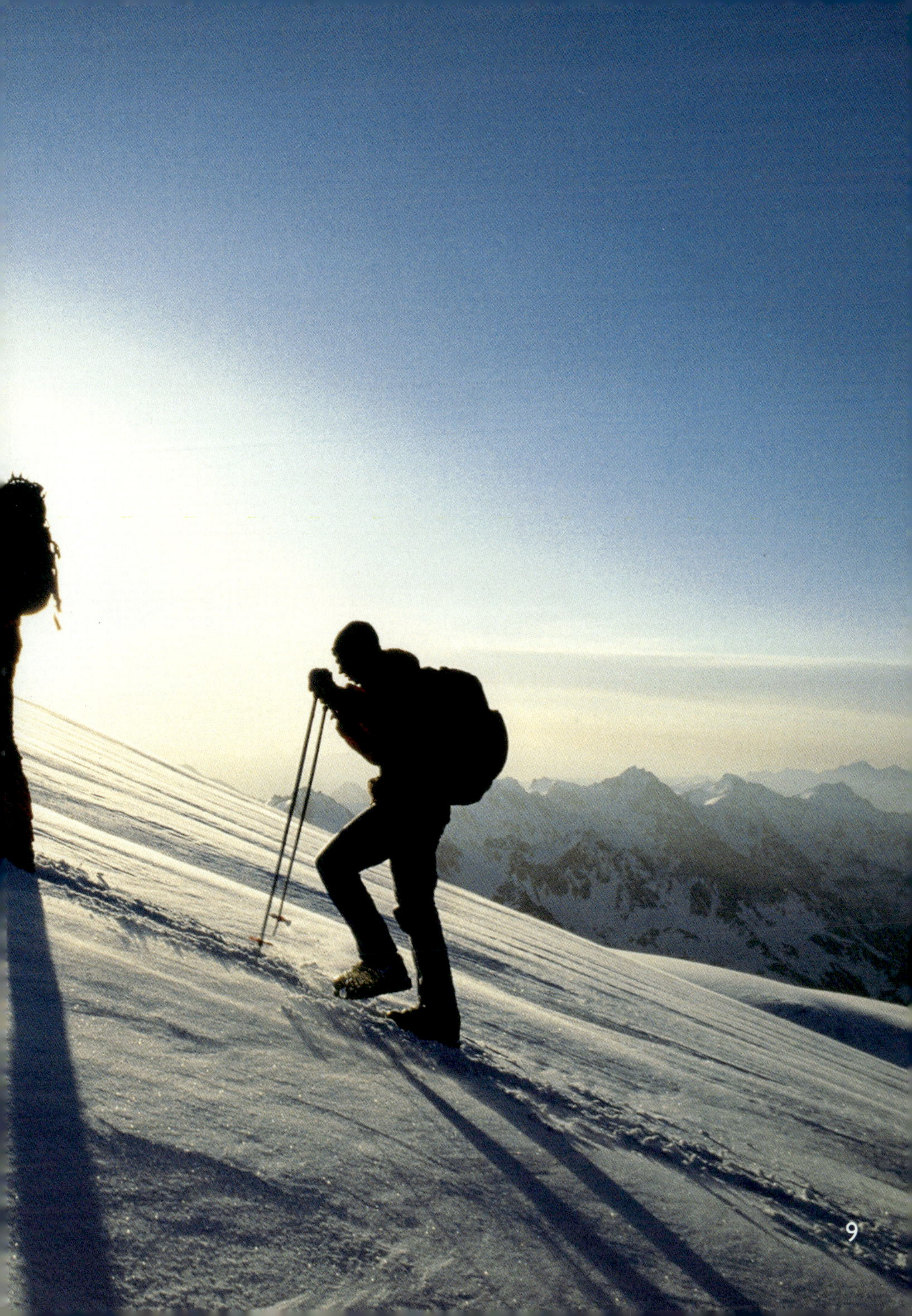

All the men wanted to be first to the top. The two strongest climbers were chosen. Hillary and Tenzing climbed together to try to reach the top of Mt. Everest.

Hillary and Tenzing

They left the last camp and climbed higher and higher all morning.
They had oxygen masks to help them breathe the mountain air.
It was hard work climbing over rocks and snow and ice.
They had to cut steps with their ice axes.

Mt. Everest

Tenzing Norgay, 1953

At last, they reached the top!
They were standing at the highest place in the world!
They put three flags in the snow to show that they had been there.

14

Nobody had ever been there before! Hillary took some photographs of Tenzing. They looked down at the other mountains. Then it was time to climb back down to their camp.

Everybody was happy when they got back. People all around the world were pleased. At last, two strong men had reached the highest place in the world.